RED SOIL - BURNING HEARTS

THE BIOGRAPHY OF A REVOLUTION

DR. RAHUL NANDIGAM

Clever Fox®
PUBLISHING
Chennai • Bangalore

CLEVER FOX PUBLISHING
Chennai, India

Published by CLEVER FOX PUBLISHING 2026

ISBN: 978-93-7500-942-9

SYMBOLIC / VISIONARY

"One book, one seed, one scream–each can start a revolution."

– Arjun,
Notes for the New Recruits

"The banyan does not grow overnight. It waits. Like us."

– Arjun, Scribbled Margin
– Red Notebook

"The soil is listening. Speak with your life."

– Arjun, Letter to Dev
(Unsent)

CONTENTS

CHAPTER ONE

PRESENT DAY – A CAMERA RETURNS (DUAL TIMELINE INTRODUCTION)

> *"The forest does not forget itsfallen. It shelters their names in the soil, and when the time is right– it sings them back into fire."*
>
> **– Arjun, Prison Diary, Page 18**
>
> *"We were never trying to win a war. We were planting seeds in ashes– so our children would grow where we once burned."*
>
> **– Excerpt from Arjun's last letter to Meera**

The van moved like a ghost, smooth and silent, beneath Bastar's emerald canopy. From the skies above, it looked like peace had returned to the forest–but peace here was always a mask. The trees remembered. The soil remembered.

The documentary crew arrived in a drone van, smoothly navigating through the lush green canopy of Bastar. The forest, which had previously been marked by violence and destruction, now appeared to be in a false state of tranquillity. The trees seemed to share their stories, and the land still resonated with past sounds. And today, a camera had come to remember too.

A woman waiting near a weathered mud-plastered brick schoolhouse, *Meera,* now silver-haired, pinned back, her face etched with both age and defiance, her jaw sharp with memory. Meera, once a revolutionary's comrade, is now a school matron and guardian of forgotten truths. She did not wave at the camera crew. She simply watched, as if weighing whether they were worthy of the story they came to dig up.

The host, young and polished, stepped out with a microphone in hand. "We're standing at what was once a rebel hideout," she asked, turning towards her. "Who was *Arjun*?"

Meera didn't look at her; instead, she gazed at the horizon before replying, her voice low but clear:

"A boy who dared to answer history with love," she said. Then, after a pause, "and with fire, when love was no longer enough."

They followed her through the school courtyard. Children sat in circles, reading passages from Arjun's red-bound diary. Some recited poems aloud, while others traced his words in chalk along the bricks salvaged from prison walls. One girl read:

"If silence is forced upon us, let us reply in thunder."

The camera panned across elderly rebels tilling the fields. One woman carried a rifle on her back and a hoe in her hand, while another cradled a child and recounted stories of Tara and the lost banyan tree.

Veena's grave rested beneath a tall neem tree, adorned with marigolds and chalk drawings made by her students. One child had written in uneven letters: "I teach because she did."

In Raipur, Dev– having hair thinner, but his eyes are as fierce as ink. He operated a modest printing press called JanSwar: The People's Voice. The shelves of the printing press overflowed with resistance literature and underground zines. When the camera crew arrived, he turned away.

"I have already taken too much of the spotlight once," he said. "Now, I just keep the ink warm."

He handed them a pamphlet titled: "The Soil That Sang."

As the film neared its closing scene, the camera ascended above the jungle, unveiling a new statue erected at the site of the first battle that had erupted years earlier. The statue depicted Arjun, his arm raised not in anger, but in a gesture of offering– holding a book in one hand and a seed in the other.

At the base, words are inscribed in four different languages.

"Leaders do not die; they multiply."

As the screen faded to black, the sounds lingered–distant drums from a tribal village, the ringing of a school bell, and the laughter of children.

The past has not ended.

It had taken root.

It was growing.

CHAPTER TWO

THE RED WOUND

RAW & PERSONAL (GRIEF / TRAUMA)

> *"Some wounds don't bleed to be seen. They burn under the skin, red as memory, slow as justice."*
>
> **– Arjun, Prison Diary – Page 43**

The sun rose over the red soil of Bastar, resembling a wound that was gradually weeping light.

In the hamlet of Bhairavpur, the village Pachgaon was already stirring. Ten-year-old Birju walked barefoot alongside his mother as they made their way to the river.

She washed clothes in silence, her eyes fixed on the tree where, just a week ago, her brother-in-law had been hanged by the landlord's men. The banyan tree, with its gnarled limbs twisted like agony made manifest in bark, would later be known as the Witness Tree.

"Why do they hate us?" Birju asked.

His mother didn't respond. Her tears were concealed by the river's current.

Later, she handed Birju a tattered schoolbook from beneath her shawl. "You must read, even if no one teaches you."

That night, the sky erupted with screams.

A wedding turned into a funeral. The bride was taken, first by the landlord, and then by the landlord's guards. The groom, a soft-spoken farmer's son, attempted to intervene. He was later found hanging from the same tree.

Birju witnessed everything, and from that moment on, his childhood came to an abrupt end.

He remained silent for several days.

In the days that followed, the red soil appeared to darken as Birju grew. He often scooped it into his palms, watching it crumble. "They think this soil forgets," he whispered. "But it remembers. Just like me."

Villagers claimed that the tree wept at night. The elders placed stones beneath it–not for worship, but as a means of remembrance. It served as a silent archive.

The first words Birju ever carved into the bark with a rusted nail were these:

"This wound is red, but it does not belong to me alone."

He returned every year on the anniversary of the wedding-that-wasn't, lighting a candle beneath the tree. The flame flickered against the bark like a breath–like a form of resistance.

The Witness Tree would eventually fall during 'Operation Dhwast'.

But before that, it stood through seasons of silence and rage.

And Birju, who would become its echo.

CHAPTER THREE

A HUNGER FOR NAMES

School was never real.

Birju etched letters into clay walls, guided by a cousin who could barely read. He used stones as makeshift chalk and a hope as his desk. His father toiled in fields he did not own–fields that consumed his sweat and yielded only hunger. Once, he was whipped for asking for water, and the scar never left his back, nor did it leave Birju's mind.

The Eye of the Bird

Weeks later, a traveling teacher arrived, a woman with dust on her saree and fire in her eyes. She carried a tin box filled with broken chalk and a pocket-sized Constitution. She gathered the children beneath the neem tree and began to teach. Thus, igniting them with the spark of knowledge.

The children sat cross-legged beneath the banyan tree, their backs warmed by the sun and their eyes fixed on the woman before them. The village teacher sat on a low wooden stool, her dupatta pinned back like a warrior's sash. The wind stirred the chalk dust from the blackboard behind her, and somewhere in the fields, a bird sang–a shrill, fluted note that seemed to pierce through the past.

The teacher opened a thin, worn book with a red cloth cover.

"Today," she said, her voice carrying across the clearing, "I will tell you of Arjuna in Mahabharata."

Young Birju, not yet the boy with a wound in his heart or a cause in his hands, looked up. He didn't like his name much. It was too soft, he'd once thought. Too sacred for someone born in the mud. But he listened.

"This Arjuna," the teacher began, "was not born into hardship. He was a prince. One of five brothers–the Pandavas. But even in privilege, he practiced more than any of them. He trained under **Guru Dronacharya**, a great master of weapons and wisdom."

She stood and picked up a branch, sketching the outline of a bow in the dirt. "The Kauravas and Pandavas–hundreds of royal cousins–were all taught by the same guru. One day, Drona decided to test them."

The children leaned closer.

"Dronacharya placed a wooden bird on the branch of a tree and called the princes one by one. 'Tell me,' He asked each student, 'what do you see?'"

She turned to a boy in the front row. "You. What would you say?"

The boy shrugged, shy. "I'd say… I see the bird."

"Good," teacher smiled as Dronacharya.

"But others said: 'I see the tree. The sky. The bird.' Even mighty Bhima said he saw the forest behind the bird."

She turned back to her story. "But when Arjuna stepped forward, he didn't blink. He drew his bow, and when asked, 'What do you see?'–

Birju raised his hand and said: *'Only the eye of the bird.'*"

She paused. Shocked, and said 'yes'.

"He didn't see distractions. Not the branches, not the leaves, not the noise of the others. Just the target. Just a purpose. And when Drona gave the word, Arjuna let the arrow fly; it struck the bird right in the eye like a flash."

The children gasped.

"Not because he had magic," the teacher said, "but because he had focus. Patience. Clarity."

Young Birju's hands tightened around his knees. He remembered watching the tree where his uncle had been hanged. How, even days later, he could see nothing else.

One day, when his uncle dared to speak out against the sarpanch, they made an example of him. They stripped him naked and marched him through the village square at noon. Men hung their heads down, women looked away, and children hid. The silence screamed louder than any whip.

Birju watched, his fists clenched so tightly that his nails broke the skin.

The next day after class, when the children ran off to play with sticks and chase goats, he lingered.

"Did Arjuna ever stop?" he asked.

The Teacher smiled. "No. Not even when the world turned against him, He fought not for fame, but for dharma–justice. Balance."

"Then I want to be Arjuna too," the boy said, the name suddenly heavy with meaning.

"Arjun," he whispered, as if casting a spell, as if making a promise. A promise that they would not erase him. That even if they buried his body, his name would remain anchored in something far stronger.

She was the first to address him by his new name, her voice firm like a verdict.

The Teacher touched his head gently. "Then keep your eyes on what matters. Not fear. Not revenge. Just the truth."

"Your name is Arjun. Wield it like a weapon."

That night, beneath the neem tree outside their hut, he carved a single word–his name–into the bark with a rusted sickle.

She taught letters as if they were tools. Vowels transformed into rallying cries, while consonants snapped like slingshots. Every sentence she uttered served as both a lesson and a revolution.

"Every name carries a lineage," she said. "Take yours back."

Under her guidance, Arjun began writing his name not only on bark but also in the air, in the soil, and in the silence of stolen nights. He inscribed it where the soldiers couldn't see it–until the day he made them aware.

The neem tree aged gracefully, its letters etched into the bark. Though they faded, they never truly vanished.

Like him, they persevered.

CHAPTER FOUR

FESTIVAL OF SMOKE

> *"We came to dance. They came to erase. But the fire they lit only cleared the mist."*
>
> **– Arjun, Festival Diary**
>
> **– Aftermath**

The event arrived like the first rain following a drought–expected, happy, and holy. The Jaatra was more than just a festival in Arjun's village of Pachgaon, which sits among red laterite earth and thick Sal trees; it was the one time each year the people laid down their daily responsibilities and gathered beneath the banyan tree to remember who they were.

The women dying bhandi and gonda fabrics in rich indigo, ochre, and scarlet for weeks before the full moon. The air re smelt like resin, smoke, and turmeric. Their fingers callused from years of both work and axe, the men fashioned wooden masks–tigers, deer, owls, and ancestors.

Arjun's mother put a scarlet thread around his wrist and neem-based oil on his hair the evening before the celebration.

"Remember the story of Veer Raja," she said, eyes softening. "We dance not for the gods but for our land, so it remembers us when others try to erase us."

The scene was bathed in a warm glow as the sun broke through the morning mist. The air was filled with energy as the drums began to play a steady, deliberate rhythm. Wearing their Warli adornments with pride, the locals emerged from their houses one by one, eager to welcome the day. Arjun wore a headband with peacock feathers, a cotton dhoti and a waistcoat that his sister had sewn. He treasured the bamboo flute that his late grandfather had given him. The shaal, which is two meters long and one metre wide, is typically worn by men. Shaals with aal-dyed red yarn and off-white ornamental weft decorations are occasionally required for festivals and ceremonial occasions. The Phenta, a turban-shaped garment that is approximately 3.5 meters long and 15 to 18 inches wide, was also frequently worn by men. It is common practice to decorate this item and reserve it for special occasions. The dhoti, a simple white shirt with a delicate red border, was worn by men in a multitude of styles as a bottom garment. When paired with an angoccha and kurta, it becomes a more festive ensemble.

The two types of patas worn by women, known as "chendra" and "ganthi marna," do not require a blouse or underskirt respectively. The everyday chendra style leaves the right shoulder exposed. It comprises tucking in the ends of the fabric and rolling it around the waist to form a waistline. The front flap, which may be used as a storage compartment for grains or fruits, is conveniently located in this design. An adjustable wrap around the mid-calf is a part of both styles. This ganthi marna style is ideal for wearing outside; to make it more covert, fasten it to the right shoulder's front flap after wrapping it around the torso, leaving one end loose at the back. There was a complete crush on the square by midday. At the outset of Song of the Forest, more dancers were present than anybody could have imagined. The women's voices floated like birds as they sang about harvests and lost lovers, while the older men played big skin drums. Exuberant with joy, the kids dashed beneath the mango-leaf decorations. However, that was short-lived. A helicopter emerged, a metallic insect with whirling wings, just as evening stained the heavens a bruised purple. Its shadow lay across the mahua tree.

Then arrived the vehicles. Green, splattered with mud and unwanted.

The paratroopers concealed their faces with black scarves and weapons thrown carelessly, as though they were there for competition.

The drummers stopped and so singing.

Arjun remained motionless with his flute in hand.

The commanding commander gave commands on bark. His voice grated against the national anthem, strange in the dialect of the plains. The issue was as old as the ground: suspicion of "Naxal gatherings," charges spun from ignorance and fear.

"This is not allowed." Spread.

The throng stood strong. An older person came up with open hands. Words flown–pleas for understanding, for respect.

A rifle butt later knocked him down.

A gulp and a scream. Children fled, tears streaking their painted faces. Women hid the elderly. Hissing, smoke bombs arced into the square, choked and blinded. Grey clouds.

Arjun gasped, eyes blazing. He watched the mahua garlands being ripped down and the holy masks crushed beneath boots. Now the 'Festival of Life' was a 'Festival of Smoke'.

Through the blur, Arjun saw his sister clutching their mother while they both coughed violently. The flute fell from his fingers. Something broke inside of him.

Burning hotter than the smoke was the question, "Why?"

Later that night, after the troops had left behind bloody ground and broken drums, Arjun returned to the area. He carried his shattered flute and a headband now ash-stained.

The community gathered peacefully under the faint moon. Now sporting a bloodied bandage, the older man spoke with mournful weight.

"They will not stop," he said. Neither of us will forget, though.

Arjun's chest seemed to be a drum pounding. The young man who loved flutes, parties, and stories began to change at that very moment. The ground had called him, and today it called something more than song.

The smoke would go. The earth would remember. And he would also performnicely.

CHAPTER FIVE

THE RIVER TOOK HER NAME

> *"She crossed the bridge, trusting it would hold. It didn't. And I have not trusted promises since."*
>
> **– Arjun, Diary**
>
> **– Year Zero**

The rain came early that year. Heavy and relentless, they pounded the red soil until it bled rivers. The Sal trees whispered with soaked leaves; the streams swelled into torrents. The village of Pachgaon became an island surrounded by water and mud.

But life could not stop. Not even in the rain.

The wooden bridge across the Sitanadi–an old, rickety thing of bamboo and rope–was the only way to reach the upper hamlets where the grain was stored. It had survived many storms. This time, it would not.

I

That morning, Meena insisted on going.

"If we don't fetch the grain now, we'll have nothing left when the soldiers come again," she said, braiding her hair quickly.

Arjun tried to stop her. "The river's too wild. Wait another day."

But Meena only smiled. "You always say wait. If we keep waiting, we'll drown in fear instead."

She wrapped herself in a faded green shawl and set off with two other women. The rain had eased, a false peace in the storm's eye. Arjun watched her go, unease coiling in his chest. But the revolution taught hard lessons: one cannot chain the brave.

II

By midday, the clouds returned, dark and pregnant with rage. Thunder rolled over the hills. The river, already swollen, roared louder.

Arjun was in the schoolhouse, helping Comrade Tara prepare leaflets, when a boy burst in, face pale.

"The bridge... It's gone. They were crossing... they..."

Arjun's heart stopped. His legs moved before he thought.

He ran through sheets of rain, feet skidding in the mud, lungs burning. When he reached the riverbank, a crowd had gathered, huddled under tarps and trees.

The bridge was no longer a bridge–only broken ropes whipping in the current. Bamboo poles bobbed like drowning limbs.

"Meena!" he shouted, voice raw.

A woman, soaked and trembling, clutched his arm. "She was in the middle when it snapped. We saw her fall. We tried to throw a rope, but... the river is too strong."

Arjun staggered to the edge, eyes wild.

"MEENA!"

No answer.

Only the river's endless roar.

III

They found her downstream hours later, tangled in roots near a bend where the water slowed. Her shawl was gone. Her braid had come loose, strands flowing like dark weeds.

Arjun waded in himself, numb to the cold, and lifted her gently from the water.

Her face was pale, peaceful–as if sleeping beneath glass. But her hands were empty. Her breath was gone.

Tara arrived in silence. Together, they carried her back through the rain.

No guns had been fired. No soldiers had come. But this too was a war–a war against nature, against poverty, against the slow violence of neglect.

A proper bridge could have saved her. Roads could have saved her. But the State had left them to drown.

IV

That night, beneath a tarpaulin strung between trees, they laid Meena's body out. The woman washed her with warm water and turmeric. Arjun sat beside her, broken flute in hand, red thread wound around his wrist.

"Forgive me," he whispered. *"I told you to be brave. I should have built you a better bridge."*

His mother wept silently, rocking beside the bier.

- Tara placed a hand on Arjun's shoulder.

"The river took her body. But the fight she carried–you must carry now."

V

At dawn, they lit her pyre beside the river. Smoke rose into a bruised sky.

As the flames burned, Arjun tied another red thread around his wrist–this one torn from her shawl, found caught in the roots where they'd pulled her from the water.

"You walked into the river for us all," he said. *"Now I will walk into the fire."*

When the rains ended and the land dried once more, Arjun began speaking in new ways. Not just of soldiers or guns, but of bridges, of roads, of justice long denied.

Revolution, he learned, is not only fought in forests with bullets. It is also fought in villages with bridges that do not break.

And in the river's roar, whenever the rain returned, he would hear her name.

> *"Her scream ended in water. Mine still echoes in the soil."*
>
> **– Arjun,**
> **First Monsoon Without Meena**

CHAPTER SIX

VEENA'S CLASSROOM

Under the shade of an ancient banyan tree, Veena taught not only letters but also land rights, caste resistance, and women's autonomy. Her classroom had no walls–only the expansive canopy of the tree she affectionately named *"The People's Canopy."*

"Under this tree," she would say, her voice resonating like a bell in the monsoon air, "No one is low. Only the branches bend." Not here either.

Children swarmed to her like moths attracted to a flickering lamp. They learnt to count not just numbers but also the wrongs they encountered, carved letters into the red earth with sticks, and chanted songs of resistance.

The people started murmuring: a revolution was under slow formation.

The landlord dispatched his guys to threaten her when he felt his hold slacken. Arriving with batons and threatening comments. Veena faced them with fierce resolve in her eyes.

She said, standing between them and her students, *"You fear knowledge more than you fear bullets."*

Her books were ripped up, the pages strewn like wounded birds. She gathered them that evening and painstakingly sewed each ripped page back together by candlelight.

But one morning, as dawn broke with a golden indifference, they caught her in the village square. They attempted to strip her before the crowd–an act intended to humiliate, dominate, and erase her identity.

Her shawl fluttered in the wind like a tattered flag, yet she stood tall and unmoving. It was her eyes, not her body, that shamed them.

Among the crowd stood Arjun, fire already etched into his bones. He screamed and picked up a stone, hurling it with all his might. Blood bloomed on a guard's forehead like a curse made manifest.

Something ancient has shattered.

The villagers, who had remained silent for too long, began to stir. First one, then many. Sickles were raised, and feet stomped the soil. Cries erupted–not of fear, but of reclamation.

That day, the village stood tall. It blazed with truth.

The banyan tree stood as a witness.

Long after the soldiers returned, they found only ash where chalk had once danced.

But the children remembered, and so did the roots.

CHAPTER SEVEN

FIRE IN THE RICE FIELDS

> *"One book, one seed, one scream–each can start a revolution."*
>
> **– Tara,**
> **Notes for the New Recruits**

They set fire to five houses that night.

It began with a rusted jeep filled with men in both uniforms and plain clothes. The land dispute had been brewing for weeks, but this was an ambush disguised as an eviction.

Children cried beneath their cots. The scent of scorched grain mingled with the wails of a newborn whose mother had barely finished delivering before being dragged into the street.

The police stood by, with one constable even laughing.

Veena clutched a ledger–the community school register, close to her chest as she ran through the haze, her heart pounding like a stampede of cattle. Behind her, their thatched hut crumbled into embers.

She fled into the forest, with Arjun in pursuit, blood trickling from a shallow cut on his brow.

First Contact with the Red Camps

They moved silently through the tall grass, deeper into the shadows. Veena stumbled over a tree root, and Arjun caught her, holding her hand longer than necessary.

A call echoed–a hoot–three times. Then, a figure stepped from behind the trees, rifle slung and eyes wary.

"Identify yourself," the woman commanded. "Now."

"I'm Arjun," he replied. "This is Veena. They burned down our homes."

The figure nodded once and said,

They navigated through a labyrinth of vines and foliage. At last, they arrived at the camp, concealed beneath a tarp and camouflaged by the red soil. Men and women sat in a circle, repairing radios, assembling leaflets, and loading ammunition.

One woman stood apart–Comrade Tara. Her eyes were as hard as stone.

"Revolution," she said, "is a slow fire. You stoke it with memory."

The Camp Stories

Each camp had its unique story.

A structure was erected near a dried-up well, where a woman had drowned for defying a priest. Another was built beneath a collapsed temple, which now serves as a classroom of dissent. Children learned mathematics alongside rifles.

Widows conducted tactical drills. Former students wrote pamphlets by moonlight. Farmers held clandestine meetings, wielding machetes and manifestos alike.

Tara presented Arjun with a map.

"They think we are a jungle, but we are a complex geography.

He nodded, and his memory ignited.

He would write no poems tonight, only plans.

CHAPTER EIGHT

DEV, THE WORDSMITH

> *"In a world that burned our books and buried our names, he printed memory into margins and called it resistance."*
>
> **– Arjun,**
> **Final Camp Diary**

Dev hailed from Raipur–tall, wiry, and perpetually carrying a satchel filled with banned books and smuggled ink. He had been arrested at seventeen for a poem titled "Rice Soaked in Blood," a poignant verse addressing hunger riots where grain was allocated by caste and silence.

He quoted Neruda and Kabir in the same breath, seamlessly blending the mystic with the militant.

"Words," he once said, "are the only ammunition that never runs out–unless we forget how to use them."

When Arjun first met him, it was in a jungle classroom constructed of mud walls and thatched leaves. Dev sat cross-legged before a circle of barefoot children and former fighters, reciting a poem while drying mimeographed leaflets over a fire.

"Who is this man?" Arjun asked Tara.

"A weapon," she replied, "honed by rejection."

Dev embraced Arjun as the brother he had never had. "You fight with your fists. That's good. Now, learn to fight with your words."

Together, they printed pamphlets on cloth, aware that the rains would dissolve paper. Although the ink occasionally ran, the messages remained intact. They translated revolutionary texts into tribal dialects and painted slogans on rocks and trees. They constructed a bamboo radio tower, transmitting stories into the night–tales of vanished fathers, imprisoned sisters, and mothers who nourished rebels while the entire world turned a blind eye.

Dev refused to communicate solely through slogans.

"Violence isn't our goal," he often told young recruits. *"It's the language imposed upon the unheard. If we can be heard–truly heard–we can choose a different narrative."*

Late into the night, he and Arjun would compose songs by candlelight, their shadows dancing on the walls like Specters of the future. One of these songs became a favourite in the movement:

If I can't write my name,
I'll write my story in fire.
Let them erase the paper
We'll carve memory into the pyre.

The song spread from forest to field, sung in secret in urban slums and whispered through prison bars.

In time, Arjun began keeping a diary–not to glorify war, but to humanize those who waged it. Dev read it often, smiling quietly. "You're a better writer than I am," he admitted once. "You still believe these words can create something meaningful."

Dev never stopped writing, not even after the betrayals, not after the burnings, and not after his lungs grew weak from inhaling smoke and lies.

And when they attempted to forget him, his verses endured–taped to school walls, woven into memory camps, and chanted by children who had never seen his face.

They were aware of his name.

He had written it down.

CHAPTER NINE

TARA'S BACKSTORY – THE STRATEGIST'S SCAR

> *"She never cried. Not because she couldn't, but because tears reveal your position."*
>
> **– Arjun, Training Notes**
>
> **– On Comrade Tara**

Before she took on the magnificent title of *Comrade Tara*–a name that sent thrills down the spines of para-military officials and inspired reverence among rebels–she was simply Tara, a vibrant child with hair shining from river play, callused feet, and an unquenchable curiosity. Her days were occupied with stories spun around the twisted roots of old banyan trees and the monsoon pulse. Born in a little woodland community close to *Konta*, her environment, albeit small, was bursting with vivid events. Her parents were carpenters and midwives. As her father, *Lalram*, deftly created wooden wheels for oxcarts that would last, the air smelt strongly of fresh wood shavings. The nighttime chorus of forest critters accompanied the soft bubbling of rice boiling in a pot, mixed with the earthy aroma of her mother's herbal concoctions. She tried to imitate her bigger brother Nandu's flute sounds with a hollow reed, while he gently named her "Choti," always allowing her to claim victory in their fun races up the neem tree. Laughing rang throughout the twilight.

But one fatal summer, a cyclone of change started to gather. One tipping point was the corruption around food supplies. The people worked long hours in serpentine queues and got little ruined rice; the rest vanished into thin air without explanation. Tara watched as Nandu painstakingly tallied the missing sacks at a community meeting; his voice grew in protest as he challenged, *"Do you expect us to starve in silence?"*

Then the *timber contractors* arrived. They took more than trees–they took schoolbooks to burn for cooking, trampled vegetable plots, and handed out bottles of local arrack like apologies. When Tara's father refused to give up the teak grove behind their hut, men came at night and torched it. The next morning, he found a dead pigeon nailed to his door.

Still, they stayed.

But it was the *first assault* that broke something. A girl named *Rekha*, barely older than Tara, had gone to fetch water and didn't return. They found her–bruised, clothes torn, half-alive in the underbrush. The CRPF patrol blamed the Naxals. The sarpanch blamed the girl. And Rekha's father drank himself to death within the month.

Tara heard her mother whisper that night, *"We cannot even bury our daughters without shame."*

It didn't end.

A borewell collapsed, killing two boys. No one came to repair it.

A teacher was arrested, accused of "brainwashing" children with poems.

A shrine was desecrated–its stones repurposed for the new CRPF outpost built on tribal farmland. When villagers protested, the officer in charge laughed: *"Gods don't need land deeds."*

A meeting was held in the village in the village center. Nandu had questioned the sarpanch again–this time in front of villagers.

The sarpanch had smiled too politely. The constable on duty narrowed his eyes.

That night, there was no knock on the door; masked men kicked down their door, tied Nandu's hands with rope.

They broke down the door, shattering the clay water pot and the silence in equal measure. Her parents begged, offering money they didn't have, swearing loyalty they didn't feel. But Nandu was dragged out–barefoot, shirtless, coughing from the dust.

For three days, the village pretended nothing had happened.

On the fourth, they found his body nailed to a tree beside the river. His fingers were broken; his flute shattered beneath him.

No one claimed the body. Only her mother, who howled like an animal as Lalram held her up. But that day, she lost her world-brother, and her parents collapsed beside Nandu's body.

Tara watched it all, frozen. She wanted to scream. To fight. But her limbs felt like stone, and her voice was buried under waves of fear.

But Tara did not cry, not even once. She buried them, and along with them, buried her innocence and fear.

That night, she did something that no one expected.

She walked quietly to their family's tools shed. She took her father's sickle, still sticky from sugarcane, and cut off her braid. She tied it to the Sal tree like an oath. Then, clutching her brother's broken flute, she tucked it into her satchel.

She turned to the shadowy forest.

And walked into it.

She left behind not just a village carrying a piece of herself– soft, wide-eyed, hoping for fairness and justice.

She followed paths her ancestors once took for gathering honey and herbs, yet now they led to whispers, to hiding places, to *others like her.*

The forest gave her no comfort at first. Only leeches, wet socks, and the uneasy breath of tigers. But she kept walking. She followed rumours of camps hidden under roots, of people who spoke in whispers and trained in silence.

And they found her.

A girl with quiet rage barely contained, clutching a rusting sickle in one hand and a battered flute in the other.

Others who had lost brothers.

Others who had nothing left to bury.

In the camps, she did not ask for a gun. She asked for a map.

She did not speak loudly, yet her eyes noted every shift of stance. She listened. And over time, when she finally spoke, quieter than the wind, they heard a certainty that folded fear into purpose; she became the one they listened to.

They called her *Comrade Tara.*

The First Fire

Tara joined the resistance not with weapons, but with ledgers. Her role was in logistics. She mapped water routes and marked old tribal paths, memorizing every armoury rotation she overheard.

But strategy came naturally to her. While others spoke of vengeance, she calculated her next move.

One ambush near the Malkangiri check post changed everything. She noticed a pattern in the convoy timings–Tuesday at noon and Saturday at dusk. She planned to create a decoy fire upstream, luring the soldiers into the marsh.

It was successful. For the first time, they didn't merely survive; they triumphed.

Tara was seventeen years old.

Scar and Silence

At eighteen, she was captured during a peace negotiation that turned into a trap.

I was interrogated for six days.

During interrogation, "Why are you fighting?"

She looked him in the eye and said:

"Because your silence made me a soldier."

On the third day, they branded her shoulder with a hot iron rod in the shape of a state seal.

She didn't scream; she simply memorized every face in the room.

On the sixth night, another detainee, an elderly Gond woman, died in her arms. "Don't let them steal our silence as well," she had whispered.

That night, Tara escaped by feigning death. She crawled through the sewage and disappeared into the hills.

She returned with a new name, a scar she never concealed, and a fury honed into strategy.

Becoming the Mind of the Movement

Comrade Tara constructed the map rooms underground and transformed abandoned temple corridors into war libraries. Every operation reflected her reasoning–bloodshed was to be avoided, but if it became necessary, it should be rendered meaningful.

To her fighters, she stated:

"We are not terrorists; we are cartographers of justice. Every step we take creates a counter-map to the State."

To her younger recruits, she provided three essential rules:

1. Always be aware of the exit before the entry.
2. Never resort to killing if you can persuade or convert instead.
3. Study your enemy's language more thoroughly than your own.

She never married, but she kept a letter written in a trembling hand folded in her pocket.

"Dear Tara, wherever you are, we remember you. Your brother's voice still echoes in our hearts."

Signed, the villagers of *Konta*.

Campfire Meeting

Now, beneath a crimson moon, she sat before Arjun and Veena.

"The revolution isn't about bullets and blood," she said. "It's about memory, discipline, and a fire that knows when to burn and when to warm."

Arjun gazed at her scar–the branded seal–while Veena gently touched her own fresh wound.

Tara handed Arjun a book with a red cover.

"Write for the ones who can't. But fight like the ones who must."

The jungle wind stirred, and a new fire was ignited.

CHAPTER TEN

FIRST STRIKE, FIRST SCHOOL

> *"The first time I pulled the trigger, my hands trembled. Not because I was afraid to kill– But because I was afraid, I might feel nothing at all."*
>
> **– Arjun, Red Sal Notebook**
>
> **– First Operation**

The camp was a whispering fire, where shadows moved with rifles and pamphlets.

Arjun sat alone, his hands stained with ink and mud. The red-bound book that Tara had given him was now half-filled with diagrams of ambush sites, *quotes from Frantz Fanon,* and verses scrawled during sleepless nights. But tonight, the ink paused.

"Comrade," Tara said, approaching silently. "It's time."

The First Operation – Broken Bridge Ambush

The target was a bridge undergoing renovation–strategically important for military movement and resented by villagers who had lost their farmlands due to its construction.

Veena insisted on conducting reconnaissance.

"They're not just soldiers there," she cautioned. "There are civilians as well. We cannot create martyrs from the wrong side."

Tara nodded. "Then we strike before dawn, when it's metal, not men."

Arjun, his rifle slung awkwardly, crouched alongside others behind the sal trees. He felt unprepared; his heartbeat echoed louder than the sounds of the forest.

"Breathe," whispered Comrade Ishaan. "Revolutions tremble before they march."

They moved. Timers were set. The plastic explosives were attached to iron bolts. Arjun's role was to provide rear support–watching for signals and covering exits.

Then, a snap. A soldier. It was too early.

A shot rang out.

Arjun reacted by shielding a teenage comrade. His bullet grazed the attacker's leg, causing the soldier to scream, but he did not die.

Veena pulled both the comrade and the injured soldier behind the foliage.

"We don't kill unless we must!" she shouted. "Treat him!"

They detonated the bridge. Steel debris rained down, but there were no casualties.

Arjun's hands trembled as he carried the injured soldier back to their lines.

He had shot, but he was saved.

Veena's Classroom Under Canopy

Days later, while others sang victory songs, Veena sat beneath a sprawling banyan tree with a slate resting on her lap.

Children surrounded her–many were barefoot, and some had bandaged limbs.

"What is a word?" she asked.

"A weapon," replied one girl.

"A window," said another.

Veena smiled and said, "A world."

She taught phonetics alongside poetry and mathematics alongside rebellion. She quoted both Gandhi and Gaddar.

When a boy asked, "Can learning stop bullets?"

She replied softly, "No, but it can eliminate the need for them."

Nearby, Arjun observed her. She was barefoot, dust-streaked, and radiating with purpose.

"She is teaching all of us," he told Comrade Ishaan.

Journal Entry – Red Soil, Burning Heart

"I did not join to shoot," Arjun wrote. "I joined because I witnessed a woman undressed for her literacy. Because my father's silence was ingrained in his very bones. Today, I stood on the brink of violence–and chose to show mercy. I bled to create. I believe the fire is transforming me."

That night, Veena read his words by the campfire.

"You will write a history they cannot erase," she said.

Arjun gazed into the flames. "Not just history. A future."

> *They say the forest made me a fighter. But it was the silence in my village that loaded the bullet."*
>
> **– Arjun, Reflection in Hiding**
>
> **– Winter Camp**

CHAPTER ELEVEN

BLOOD AND ROOT

> *"We did not choose this fight. It was sown into us– rooted in blood, watered in silence."*
>
> **– Arjun, Jungle Notebook**
>
> **– Entry Before the Monsoon Raid**

The forest was no longer merely concealing them; it was listening–watchful and vigilant.

Operation *'Dhwast'* was launched in silence. There were no press releases, no alerts–only boots, jeeps, and matches.

At Bhairavpur, grain stores were set ablaze as children looked on, barefoot and gasping for air amidst the smoke. One mother, who had been teaching her daughter to count, was assaulted in front of her blackboard.

A constable laughed while another filmed.

The banyan tree, the oldest in the district, known as Vriksha-Mata, was chained and cut down. It's sap bled like a memory torn open. Villagers wept like orphans. Beneath its roots, Veena had once taught the meaning of the word "freedom."

The word burned.

The Counterstrike – Battle of Chilpathar

Arjun sits alone beneath a tree, flute in hand. The moonlight catches the *fractured wood and faded red thread.*

He closes his eyes and hears the old festival song. In his mind:

His sister's tears. His friend was dragged by troops. The elder was struck down. Smoke in the night. The broken soil.

He opens his eyes. *Resolve hardens. "For them,"* he whispers.

Arjun stood beneath the moonlight, his red scarf tied tightly.

"We strike tonight," Tara declared, her voice as resolute as steel tempered by sorrow. "Not to seek vengeance, but to remind them–we are not ash."

The target is a paramilitary outpost near Chilpathar, notorious for detaining and "disappearing" young men. Inside, there is a new shipment of arms and captives.

Their formation was tight. Veena managed the evacuation protocols, while Arjun led the central flank. Each comrade carried not only ammunition but also the names of those who had disappeared.

At 2:13 a.m., the bamboo fence burst inward.

Arjun fired, but never at the head–only at the legs to disarm and disable his targets.

One soldier, no older than him, trembled with fear. Arjun aimed the rifle, then lowered it. "Run."

The boy dropped his weapon and fled into the shadows.

Fifteen rebels fell. One grenade had landed too close. A young girl with a red bindi had smiled just before the detonation. “Tell my brother I sang,” she whispered.

They seized the post.

Meera Among the Ashes

When it was over, Arjun found her.

Meera, wounded in the shoulder and half-conscious, lay with her dark blood staining the leaves.

“Why… why do they fear the alphabet?” she murmured.

Arjun carried her in his arms; she weighed less than his guilt.

Veena met him halfway, took Meera’s hand, and whispered.

“You will teach again–with red ink, not red blood.”

Later, the villagers gathered around the banyan stump. Arjun etched words into its weathered bark:

“You chopped the branches, but forgot, the roots teach resilience.”

In the morning, the children sat in a circle.

Class has resumed.

CHAPTER TWELVE

MEERA'S MISSION

> *"She was not chasing glory. She was planting truths where lies had taken root."*
>
> **– Tara's field notes, final page**

Meera had arrived from Delhi, her suitcase packed with law books, idealism, and a conviction that democracy required only better advocates. She was young then–barely twenty-four–equipped with degrees from prestigious universities and a certain naive disbelief.

"I came to teach them about their rights," she told Arjun later, "but they taught me how to survive without them."

At first, she attempted to establish legal clinics beneath banyan trees, providing villagers with guidance on land claims and constitutional protections. She cited specific clauses, referenced Supreme Court rulings, and even filed petitions. However, each document vanished into the bureaucracy like leaves in a monsoon drain.

The people smiled politely but continued to hand her stories instead of affidavits: tales of vanished daughters, scorched harvests, and men beaten for drinking water from the wrong well.

One day, the stories finally caught up to her.

The landlord's men approached her as she walked back from a village meeting to Chilpathar. They were masked, armed, and laughing. They dragged her to the village square, where they tore her salwar and paraded her like a trophy–a warning to others.

She fought fiercely, biting one of her attackers and spitting in another's face. However, there were too many of them.

They took her to the nearby paramilitary outpost–a crumbling building that was once intended for protection but has now become a den of fear. The soldiers did not intervene; they merely watched.

When Arjun and his unit arrived that night, they moved like smoke–unseen and unrelenting. From the darkness of the jungle came a rain of bullets and machetes. The landlord's men fell before they could even scream. By dawn, the outpost was silent.

On its gates, they left a letter written in red:

"Touch the people again, and we'll bring war to your doorstep."

Inside, they found Meera–bloodied, her shawl torn, and her eyes ablaze.

Arjun offered her a blanket, but she refused. She stood tall, her chest heaving and trembling–but unbroken.

"They may undress our bodies," she said through gritted teeth, "but they will never strip our cause."

That night, she joined the armed wing–not as a fighter, but as a Firestarter.

She shaved her head and wrapped her wrists in red thread. She ceased quoting laws and began rewriting them on walls. She collected coal from the burned schoolhouses and painted slogans across village walls, police checkpoints, and ration centers:

"We are the law."

"If your court won't hear us, the forest will."

She became known in hushed tones. No longer as a teacher, but as Adhikar Didi–the Sister of Rights.

Meera never forgot Delhi; she simply stopped waiting for its justice to arrive.

Instead, she created her own.

CHAPTER THIRTEEN

MEERA'S AWAKENING (PREQUEL ARC)

> *"You don't wake up all at once. You notice the bruises, the hunger, the lies, And one day, you stop looking away."*
>
> **– Meera, Interview Transcript (Later Years)**

Before she became a name whispered beneath the banyan leaves, before she earned the title "Mother of the Jungle Schools, Meera was a firebrand at Delhi University.

She wore simple cotton saris, with a jhola slung over one shoulder. Inside, there were always two books: the Constitution of India and the *Collected Poems of Faiz Ahmed Faiz.*

She engaged in debates with professors, marched alongside sanitation workers, and organized campus forums focused on land rights. Her candlelight vigils following custodial deaths garnered both admiration and threats. Her speeches, sharp and unwavering, possessed a cadence that compelled even her critics to pause.

At the age of 22, she became the youngest intern ever accepted at the Planning Commission's Tribal Affairs desk. This position was regarded as a stepping stone to a prestigious policy fellowship overseas.

However, Bastar derailed everything.

Bastar Internship

Sent to observe the ground-level education infrastructure, Meera arrived at an unnamed village after an eight-hour jeep ride followed by a two-hour trek.

What she discovered caused her hand to tremble.

Children with bleeding feet dig into rocky soil. There are no teachers, no blackboards, and no roof–only sticks, stones, and determination.

"There are no teachers," one boy told her, holding a rusted tin plate and a hoe. "Only soldiers."

At the edge of the clearing, two girls practiced the alphabet by tracing letters in the dirt with twigs. One of them had a fresh scar across her cheek.

That night, in her government guesthouse, Meera wrote nothing on her report form. She simply cried.

Return to Delhi

Back in Delhi, her thesis defence was attended by deans and bureaucrats. The title of her thesis was "Efficacy of State-Led Educational Interventions in Tribal Zones".

When the panel inquired about "empirical data," she froze.

Then, trembling, she spoke:

"They ask us to write reports on blood; I would prefer to learn how to stop the bleeding.

There was a prolonged silence. A professor attempted to continue, but she left the room mid-sentence.

She never returned to academia.

A New Path

She sent her fellowship rejection via email. Donated her formal wear, and moved back to Bastar with one trunk, a set of chalk, and her two books.

The Constitution. Faiz.

She began teaching under a Sal tree. She had ten students in the first week and thirty by the end of the month.

In the evenings, she wrote letters–not academic ones, but rather poems and manifestos that were sent by cycle courier to young activists throughout the country.

Her favourite line, underlined in every letter:

"We are not born radical; the world shapes us so.".

CHAPTER FOURTEEN

THE WEDDING THAT WASN'T

> *"The bells were ready, the rice was washed, But history had other plans. And joy was buried in the same ground as the groom."*
>
> **– Meera,**
> **Recounting the Ambush at Kirsar**

In the gentle haze of spring, the forest appeared more inviting.

Veena and Arjun planned their wedding like rebels–quietly, in the dappled light beneath the leaves. There were no priests, no rituals, only a promise.

Dev strung garlands from vines, while children painted pebbles with images of birds. Even Tara, who was often characterized by silence and steel, allowed herself a rare smile.

"I've seen too many funerals," she said. "Let there be joy in camouflage."

Dev composed a poem:

"Where bullets bloom,

let love be our gunpowder.

In the silence between gunfire,

let us inscribe our vows in the red soil."

That night, the fire crackled not with strategy, but with song.

Veena brushed ash from her sari and whispered to Arjun, "Will you help me build a school?"

He cupped her hands, which were scarred from training, and replied, "A hundred. And name them after the girls they silenced."

They were being watched.

A mole had whispered coordinates to the district headquarters–a betrayer among them. The cost of visibility was blood.

The Raid Before Dawn

In the gentle haze of spring, the forest seemed even more inviting.

Veena and Arjun planned their wedding like rebels–quietly, in the dappled light beneath the leaves. The ambush occurred at 3:27 a.m. It was not gunfire at first, but the sound of barking dogs and birds taking flight from the canopy, like sirens of instinct.

Then came the flashbangs. Screams erupted. Smoke grenades hissed like a melody.

Arjun grasped Veena's hand. "Get the children out!

Tara stood at the entrance of the tent, firing into the darkness. She shielded two young girls as a volley of gunfire erupted around them. Her shoulder was wounded, and she collapsed.

Arjun pulled her back; a bullet lodged in his thigh. "Tara!"

She clutched his collar, her blood pooling thickly between them.

"Create schools," she whispered. "Not graves."

Tara passed away before sunrise.

The Wedding That Became a Burial

Arjun buried her beneath the banyan tree. Now, only a stump remained, its roots exposed like nerves.

He carved her name with his bayonet, followed by Veena's beside it.

Not death. Not surrender. Only memory.

The garlands intended for Veena's wedding now adorned the rifles.

Veena stood at dawn; her face streaked with tears and mud. "From this day forward, we fight not for vengeance, but for a promise."

Arjun nodded. "For Tara. For the school where she will never teach.

The sun filtered through the leaves.

Bells intended for the ceremony were affixed to the necks of message runners. The children delivered letters to villages, announcing not a wedding, but a red resolve. In a distant location, the traitor sat in uniform, quietly weeping in a bunker.

CHAPTER FIFTEEN

THE GHOST OF BETRAYAL

> *"Trust is the only thing we buried without a grave. The traitor doesn't kill you once. He kills you every time you remember his face and call it brother."*
>
> **– Tara,**
> **Codename: Kiran Dossier**

The rain soaked the Red Camp.

Names of the fallen were inscribed on stones, which the children arranged in circles. There were no graves, only markers of memory.

Veena now walked with a limp, but her voice had only grown sharper. "No more shadows," she declared. "We will find the ghost."

Arjun discovered the journal among Tara's belongings–its pages filled with codes in Marathi, Bengali, and faded tribal dialects. Her final entry read:

"If they come for us, it will be from within."

At night, gathered around the fire, Arjun read aloud the list that Tara had compiled: cross-referenced shifts, missing rations, and changes in patrol timings. Someone had been feeding coordinates for weeks.

The Red Council convened in silence.

Dev, visibly shaken, said, "The ink is still wet. That means they are close."

A name has appeared multiple times.

Yogesh is their radio technician. He is a quiet man, an ex-constable, who often remains on the periphery of conversations.

They discovered him attempting to transmit once more.

Veena confronted him.

"Why?" she asked, lowering her rifle.

Yogesh sobbed, promising my daughter medicine. She's dying in Raipur. I... I had no choice.

No one spoke; Arjun's hands trembled.

"He still has one," Veena said as she walked away. "Let him choose."

Yogesh took his own life the following dawn, with a note tied to his chest.

"Forgive me. Let her live."

The Red Camp has burned down its old location.

By dusk, the new site was nestled deep within the Satpura jungle, intertwined with cliffs, moss, and memories. They renamed it Tara Shivir – Tara's Camp.

Children painted new signs:

"Not rebels. Roots."

And above them, etched into stone:

"One betrayal cannot erase a revolution."

CHAPTER SIXTEEN

ROOTS BEFORE THE FIRE (PREQUEL ARC)

> *"Before the slogans and the smoke, we were just children chasing monsoons, and stories growing beneath the trees."*
>
> **– Arjun, Remembering Pachgaon**

The forest was a cathedral to young Birju–a universe woven together by sacred soil, whispering streams, and towering Sal trees. Each morning, his father, Kuna Ram, would mark his brow with ash and place his hand against the bark, murmuring blessings in Gondi.

"Everything listens here," he told Birju. "Even the wind."

Kamli would laugh while grinding spices beside the hearth. "The gods live here, and they are hungry for stories."

That summer, the rains were delayed, causing the river to dwindle to a mere trickle. In this context, Darbar Singh's men arrived, posing as irrigation surveyors. Their boots splattered mud across tribal murals, while the surveyors' marked trees with bright red paint.

Kuna Ram tried to resist peacefully. He gathered village elders. "We are not tenants," he said. "We are time."

Days later, Birju returned from fetching wood to find the air thick with silence. No birds. No fire crackle. Just sobbing–raw and close. He ran.

In the courtyard, Kamli lay crumpled, her sari torn, eyes swollen shut. A young bride–Leela, newlywed–was being dragged away by Darbar's henchmen toward the zamindar's estate. His mother, bleeding from the mouth, clung to the shrine. Kuna Ram stood bloodied, head bowed, surrounded by policemen.

Darbar Singh approached. "Next time you gather a protest, I'll gather a feast."

They stripped Kamli and forced her to walk around the village circle. Kuna Ram screamed until they broke his jaw.

That night, the hut burned.

Under the stars, Birju did not cry. He dug a hole beside the banyan tree and buried the family's brass prayer bell. "I will return for this," he whispered.

CHAPTER SEVENTEEN

THE BIRTH OF COMRADE ARJUN

> *"Revolutions don't fall from the sky. They rise from soil–where love once lived, and something was taken."*
>
> **– Arjun,**
> **Page 49 Red dairy**

"You will call me Arjun," Birju said to the rebels who found him wandering the forest along with Veena.

Comrade Harish raised a brow. "Why not Bhima? You carry rage."

"I aim for eyes, not heads."

In the rebel camp, days began before sunrise. Training was ruthless. Commander Taara taught him to disassemble rifles blindfolded. Harish gave him *The Communist Manifesto* and a bamboo rod.

"You must fight with mind and muscle."

Arjun scribbled in a notebook each night:

"I was born from fire, but I do not burn randomly. I choose my flames."

Then, Veena appeared during a field exercise. Her hair tied back, eyes scanning the trees.

Comrade Harish corrected his sling posture with a touch.

"You're not aiming. You're hoping."

"I never hoped," he said. "Until now."

That evening, by the river, Veena shared her story:

"My brother tried to report the zamindar. They made him dig his own grave. I was next. But someone lit a match. Now I am wildfire."

He took her hand. "Then let us burn together."

In her, he found a mirror–not of pain, but purpose.

They led education raids together. Veena's passion was for schools–chalk and red flags. She once held a class at gunpoint in a state-run building, demanding it be turned over to tribal teachers.

"The first weapon," she'd say, "is the word."

Years passed. Arjun became the face of the revolution–feared by the State, loved by the oppressed. His unit, the *People's Liberation Squad*, struck police convoys, destroyed illegal mining camps, and protected villagers from forced displacements.

CHAPTER EIGHTEEN

ECHOES OF LIBERATION

> *"Liberation does not end with victory. It lingers in footsteps, in fields replanted, in the laughter of children who no longer hide."*
>
> **– Arjun's Speech**
>
> **– The Hilltop Gathering**

The jungle was quiet, but the silence hummed with a strange anticipation. It had been three days since Taara's death, and the forest seemed to grieve with them. Even the birds sang in minor keys.

Arjun sat beside her grave, a simple mound beneath the banyan's roots. The stump, though scarred and leafless, gave a solemn shade. He pressed his forehead to the bark.

Footsteps crunched behind him. Meera stood, a rifle slung over one shoulder, her kurta splattered with mud and dried blood. "There's movement at the southern outpost. The new commander... he's burning food caches. Children are going hungry."

Arjun turned. His face, once young, now looked carved by fire and ash. "Then we give them a memory they can't burn."

The Gathering

That night, in the dense heart of the forest, around a fire carved into the red soil like an altar, Arjun summoned the cells. Fighters and thinkers came. So did the broken: mothers who'd lost sons, students expelled for protest, widowers with no name.

"We strike at dawn," Arjun said. "But not just with bullets."

Dev stood beside him, holding a stack of cloth-bound leaflets. "We give them stories. Songs. Proof that we still speak."

"And if they crush us?" asked a young boy named Ramu.

"Then we die loud," said Meera. "So loud that even their silence echoes."

Symbolic Interlude: The Red Drum

As plans were drawn, Tara brought out an old war drum–red ochre painted in circles. "This belonged to my grandfather. He beat it during the famine riots of '42. Let it beat again."

Arjun placed his palm on it. "Let the drum remember our names."

The Assault on Bhairavpur Checkpoint

At sunrise, the forest erupted. A series of synchronized attacks rained upon the police checkpoint near Bhairavpur. Molotov met steel. Women with sharpened sickles cut through barbed fences. Songs were broadcast from stolen megaphones:

"We are the soil. You cannot erase the land."

Arjun, leading from the front, ducked behind a termite mound as bullets shattered bark. A police constable ran toward him, shouting, "I'm one of yours!"

Too late.

A loyalist shot the man in the back. Arjun turned to Meera. "Even in betrayal, they die trying to believe."

By noon, the checkpoint fell. Villagers gathered. For the first time, they saw no police.

Instead, they saw Arjun standing atop the red drum, his voice thunderous:

"This checkpoint? It belongs to you now. This land? Yours. This silence? Ours to break forever."

Children danced where soldiers once marched.

A new dawn had begun to echo.

Darbar Singh's estate fell not with an explosion but with silence.

Meera led the tribunal. Survivors testified. A young woman named Leela stood shaking.

“This man... before my wedding...” Her voice broke. But the crowd did not.

They listened. Then they acted.

Darbar begged for mercy. Meera did not smile. “Mercy is not forgetting. It’s remembering enough not to repeat.”

They hung him from the same tree where Kamli had been paraded.

Echoes

That night, Meera sat with Dev, watching the stars.

“Do you think they’ll remember us?” she asked.

Dev handed her a pamphlet, soaked slightly with blood. “If memory is rebellion, we’ve already won.”

In Panchgaon, old women painted the banyan stump red. Not with blood, with vermillion.

CHAPTER NINETEEN

MEERA'S LEGACY

> *"She stayed. Through arrests, through silence, through survival. Not all heroes carry rifles. Some carry memory."*

Now, the school having walls built from reclaimed prison bricks – remnants of a colonial jail razed during the uprising. Its foundation stone was Tara's rifle barrel, welded into the threshold.

Children sat cross-legged on woven reed mats; algebra scrawled in chalk beside revolutionary history.

"Who was Arjun?" one boy asked.

Meera paused, touched the diary on her desk.

"A boy who saw fire and became it," she said, her voice firm, reverent.

The wind carried the scent of red soil and mango blossoms. A banyan sapling – grown from the root of the original Panchgoan tree – stood tall in the courtyard, encircled by student-painted tiles.

Each classroom bore a verse on its door:

"They took our land. We planted memory."

International visitors came cautiously, some bearing agendas, others curiosity.

UN delegates arrived one monsoon afternoon, boots heavy with mud and scepticism.

A Swedish diplomat asked, “Are you still rebels?”

Meera, dressed in a handwoven sari dyed with forest indigo, pointed to the blackboard.

“Only against forgetting,” she replied.

That evening, students performed a play: *The Ballad of Tara*, set beneath an open sky. Girls carried wooden rifles; boys sang the song Dev once wrote for the wedding that wasn’t.

At the entrance of the school hung a photograph: Veena and Arjun – smoke rising behind them, smiling defiantly, arms around each other.

Next to it, a plaque read:

“This campus is carved from sacrifice. Education is our uprising.”

Meera sat in her office late one night, reviewing essays.

A girl named Sita had written:

“My mother was raped in Bhairavpur. My father never returned from the police camp. But I dream in long division and Bengali script. I dream because you stayed.”

Meera folded the paper gently. Her eyes welled.

"I didn't stay," she whispered. "I grew roots."

Outside, under the banyan, children practiced oratory for a village debate.

One boy quoted from Arjun's diary:

"If my bones feed roots, let them grow swords."

Meera smiled.

Their fire had become a light.

And the school – once born of blood – was now a garden.

CHAPTER TWENTY

THE DIARY AND THE RISING (PREQUEL)

> *"The diary was not just paper and pain. It was a matchstick buried in dry leaves. When it opened, something rose."*
>
> **– Meera,**
> **Archive Preface: The Diary and the Rising**

Meera reached the tribal hamlet of Panchgaon at dusk, her jeep covered in the reddish dust that clung like the blood of memory. The village sat quietly, the kind of silence that came from grief, not peace. Children peered from behind low mud walls, their eyes bright with hunger and caution.

"This book," she told the villagers who gathered near a dying fire, "contains the voice of Arjun."

She lifted the diary – leather-bound, frayed at the corners, its pages stained with sweat, soot, and what she could only assume was blood. Her voice trembled as she began:

"If my bones feed roots, let them grow swords."

The children sat closer. A mother hushed her baby. A boy, no older than ten, repeated the line. Then another. Soon, a ripple of voices recited it together, as if invoking a ghost.

Women painted murals of Arjun on cracked walls – him standing tall beside a broken banyan, his chest open, and from it sprouting saplings with blades for leaves. One mural showed Veena in her bloodstained shawl, her hand reaching toward children beneath the People's Canopy.

A group of youth emerged from the woods. They wore red scarves tied around their necks, a new symbol. Some carried notebooks, others slingshots. They called themselves the **Sons of the Soil**.

At Bastar's government college, classrooms buzzed. A photograph of Arjun kissing the red drum was painted in a corridor. Teachers turned a blind eye. Students lit candles below his picture and chanted:

"He died. We awaken."

At JNU, the graffiti war exploded. Over colonial pillars and glass doors, red spray-paint screamed:

"We do not inherit silence. We inherit rebellion."

"From the jungle, the nation shall rise."

"Books and bullets–he carried both."

Back in Panchgaon, an old woman wrapped in a faded sari handed Meera a cup of chai. Her hands trembled as she touched Meera's cheek.

"You are their daughter now," the woman said.

Meera looked down, unsure how to carry the weight.

"I'm no leader," she replied, her voice barely above a whisper. "Only a vessel."

The old woman smiled. "That's all Arjun was too. Vessels carry fire. Just don't let it go out."

That night, around the campfire, Meera read another passage. Arjun had written it a week before his final battle:

"If history forgets us, let it choke on our echoes. If they write us down, let it be in red."

And beneath the banyan stump, someone had left a red scarf tied to a sapling, now rising from the roots.

"The Rising had begun".

CHAPTER TWENTY-ONE

THE TRIBUNAL AND THE TRUTH

> *"In their court, the truth stood trial. In ours, it stood unshaken."*
>
> **– Meera**

Meera stood in the open-air tribunal tent, its sides flapping like restless birds. The sky above Bastar was dense with clouds, as if the land itself held its breath.

The people had gathered – tribals, students, former rebels, activists in faded kurtas, even journalists now daring enough to seek truth where only silence once ruled.

A panel of elders presided beneath a tattered tricolour, pinned between bamboo poles. The cloth barely held together – frayed at the Ashoka Chakra, like a symbol tested too long.

Photographs of the martyrs lined the tent's inner walls – black-and-white images laminated and nailed to wood. Arjun's face was at the centre, eyes defiant.

A government official in a starched white kurta leaned forward.

"Why was force the only answer?" he asked, pen trembling above a blank sheet.

Before Meera could respond, an old woman rose. Her spine bent like a question mark, hands warped by years of grinding millet and burying sons.

"Because words were buried under boots," she said. "Because we were stripped even of screams."

The statement was not rhetorical. It was historical. The silence that followed was not empty – it was reverent.

Dev sat in the rear, thinner than before, eyes hollow but present. He awaited judgment – not from law, but from memory.

Meera stepped forward. She opened Arjun's diary; its pages were weathered with sweat and time.

She read:

"They tried to silence us with hunger. But we learned to feed each other with fire."

The wind swirled through the open flaps, lifting corners of petitions, petitions that had been ignored for generations.

A child in the front row whispered, "That's his handwriting."

A young teacher translated the words into Gondi for elders in the crowd. One began to cry.

The official lowered his pen. "And now?" he asked, quietly. "Now that the guns have quieted?"

Meera looked at the crowd, then at Dev, then at the banyan sapling visible on the hill.

“Now,” she said, “we raise voices instead of rifles. But the memory remains loaded.”

The panel conferred. A ruling was delivered – not one of punishment, but of restoration.

Land would be returned. Police camps relocated. Education is declared sacred.

As the sun broke through clouds, a journalist tweeted:

Bastar breathes truth. Finally.

And in a village down the path, someone rang a school bell.

CHAPTER TWENTY-TWO

DEV'S SHADOW (PREQUEL ARC)

> *"Every revolution has its shadow– the one who writes what the fallen can no longer say."*
>
> **– Arjun,**
> **on Dev's role in The Soil That Sang**

Dev's first poem was banned before it was ever printed.

It described a mother washing blood from rice with river water that had turned rust-red.

He was seventeen.

The school expelled him. His name was erased from rosters, and his face was posted in the campus gatehouse like a criminal.

At home, his father–once a clerk at the district court–refused to speak to him. His mother wept quietly, folding his shirts with trembling fingers.

Dev left Raipur that same night with a tattered notebook and a burning in his chest.

He found refuge in underground theatre collectives, where scripts were copied by candlelight and stages were bamboo platforms hidden in mango groves. There, he met runaways, artists, and rebels who taught him that ink could become insurgency.

His most famous play, *The Banyan Burns*, opened in a half-collapsed grain warehouse. The play portrayed the systematic assault on a tribal village, its climax a funeral lit by burning textbooks. It was performed only once–before police stormed the venue and arrested everyone in attendance.

Dev spent six months in lockup. When he emerged, he was gaunt, eyes sunken, but his voice sharper.

When Arjun found him, Dev was sitting outside the Raipur general hospital, cradling a newspaper with his name misspelled in a list of released detainees.

"You write war," Arjun said.

"I write to make them uncomfortable," Dev replied, without looking up.

"Come make them afraid."

And Dev did. He travelled with Arjun into the heartland – where language was a frontline, and each sentence a weapon. His poems became songs. His manifestos turned into murals.

But one winter, his mother fell ill. Her lungs collapsed from exposure to pesticide fumes. The state offered him something he could not ignore: access to a Delhi hospital, air tanks, surgery – in exchange for a signed affidavit disowning his comrades.

He signed it.

His mother died anyway, few days later.

The affidavit was leaked. Some comrades cut all ties. Others, like Veena, never stopped speaking to him – but stopped quoting him.

Dev spent the rest of his life trying to patch the cracks in his conviction. Each article he published under his pen name, each poem smuggled into newspapers, each moment he showed up despite knowing who he had failed – was an act of contrition.

His shadow was long.

CHAPTER TWENTY-THREE

DEV'S POETRY AND BETRAYAL (PREQUEL)

> *"I wrote verses to soothe the fire– but some fires were never too calm. And some betrayals begin with silence."*
>
> **– Dev, Unpublished**

Dev was not born to violence. He was born to a weaver mother and a farmer father, under a mango tree where words outnumbered leaves.

He joined the movement not with a rifle, but a harmonium.

"I can turn wounds into music," he once said to Arjun.

"You'd better turn spies into silence," Arjun replied.

Dev sang to lull infants during midnight marches. He wrote revolutionary plays staged in jungle clearings. Veena, though sceptical, saw value.

"The children remember more from his songs than our speeches," she admitted.

But Dev's world began to tilt when his mother fell ill. Confined to a hospital in Raipur, her only chance was expensive treatment.

A CID officer named Rathi approached him. "Help us find Arjun. Save your mother."

He resisted. Then caved.

He left coded symbols near rebel camps. Used poetry readings as distractions. Sent coordinates sewn into prayer flags.

One night, staring into a campfire, he muttered, "What is betrayal if the choice is between your mother's breath and your brother's dream?"

Veena began to suspect. "Poets lie with beauty. That's why they're dangerous."

CHAPTER TWENTY-FOUR

THE BLOOD ARCHIVE

> *"This is not a record. It is a graveyard of stories, and we carry it because no one else will."*
>
> **– Meera,**
> **to her students on Archiving Day**

The forest held its breath, as if knowing that memory was about to be unearthed.

At the heart of an abandoned colonial courthouse now reclaimed by banyan roots and fireflies, Meera and Dev descended into what was once the archives room. Each step creaked, damp with time and silence.

"Arjun said this was the first place they tried to erase," Meera whispered. "So, he rewrote it."

Torchlight flickered over faded police logs, burnt petitions, and confiscated letters. In a hidden stone cavity behind a loose brick, Dev found a red tin box wrapped in wax cloth. Inside were sheaves of Arjun's handwritten letters, coded communiqués, charcoal sketches, and, at the bottom, a map soaked with red soil.

On it was a single line:

"Where blood stains the roots, memory grows."

Reconstructing the Archive

They carried the contents to a nearby schoolhouse–the very one Veena once tried to reopen. Now, it has become a library of resistance.

Meera laid out the materials on woven mats. Children sorted the papers by year. Dev digitized each document with a cracked tablet and solar panel.

Each letter was a seed.

In one, Arjun wrote:

"Veena taught me alphabet of courage. The revolution is not only a gun–it is a pen that refuses to be silent."

In another, he had drawn a diagram of the People's Canopy–a guerrilla school under a banyan, where math was taught with stones and revolution with rhythm.

Women from the village brought offerings to the schoolhouse–baskets of tamarind, rice, and red flowers. A teenage girl stood and asked Meera, "Can we call it The Blood Archive?"

Meera nodded; her voice thick. "Because every word in here was written so you wouldn't have to die for the truth again."

The First Reading

That night, under lantern glow and the canopy of stars, villagers gathered to hear the first reading. Dev stood at the front, holding Arjun's poem titled *"Soil Writes Back."*

"You brought guns,

We brought fireflies.

You stole words,

We carved them in bark.

You wrote history in steel,

We answered in . Sapling"

A hush fell. Some wept. Others began to chant the last stanza. The poem spread faster than fire.

Across the border in Dantewada, a local journalist leaked excerpts to foreign outlets. The BBC ran a piece titled: "Rebel Poet Ignites Bastar's Forgotten War."

In Delhi, a parliamentary inquiry was ordered. Not to honour Arjun–but to silence the movement.

Parallel Timeline Interlude (Modern Day)

A young filmmaker dug through old footage. Her name was Ranya–granddaughter of the officer who once led the Bastar raids.

At an independent film studio in Mumbai, a documentary team reviewed this old raw footage. One screen showed Meera reading to children. Another displayed drone shots of the jungle, the banyan stump glowing with prayer candles.

The producer turned to her assistant. "This... This isn't just a story of rebellion. This is a new constitution written in red clay."

"Do we have rights to the letters?"

"Ranya said it belongs to the people now."

The camera zoomed in on Arjun's final diary page. A smudged line barely legible:

"If even one child learns freedom, I have not died."

CHAPTER TWENTY-FIVE

VEENA'S FIRE (PREQUEL ARC)

> *"Some girls burn quietly. Veena did not. She turned her fire into a school."*
>
> **– Inscription beneath Veena Patil People's School plaque**

Veena was twelve when she saw her brother's lifeless body hanging from the fig tree outside the village square. His face had been beaten beyond recognition; his fingers were broken, and one eye was still half-open as if he had more to say.

The soldiers referred to him as a disruptor.

Her mother, kneeling in the dust, remained silent at first. Then, in a hoarse voice, she spoke:

"He taught girls how to read.

They called ita rebellion."

Veena remained silent; She neither cried nor screamed.

She picked up his old slingshot from the ground, aimed it at the setting sun, and released the stone. It didn't strike anything, but something within her shattered and ignited.

They sent her away to Dantewada soon after the incident.

Officially, she was placed with distant relatives; however, unofficially, she descended into the underground.

In the damp cellars beneath the cracked foundations of an abandoned library, Veena met Comrade Sara, not as a gun-wielding commander, but as a teacher of dangerous things.

"Revolution is not male," Sara stated, holding chalk in one hand, with an AK-47 resting beside the blackboard. "It is a language, and language can bleed."

Veena learned how to dismantle colonial syllables, remove propaganda from textbooks, and reassemble grammar that resisted.

In between coded lessons, she memorized maps, escape routes, and the art of carrying entire histories within a single folded note.

By seventeen, Veena was running a mobile school disguised as a tiffin delivery service.

Inside each metal lunchbox:

The top layer consists of roti, pickle, and lentils.

The bottom layer consists of banned books, handwritten lessons, and poems scribbled in red ink.

If she were stopped, she would say:

"I'm a maid. They don't allow me to go to the school, sir."

Sometimes the soldiers laughed. Sometimes they spit.

They never looked beneath the rice.

When she met Arjun, he was quiet but sharp-eyed, his hands stained with ink from copying pamphlets late into the night.

She asked him only one question, her expression devoid of a smile:

"Would you die to build a classroom?"

Arjun looked up and said,

"Only if I can live to teach inside it."

Years later, when the movement built its first school in the free zone, they named it in honour of her.

The Veena Patil People's School.

The sign was carved in Gondi, Hindi, and English.

And beneath it, someone had painted in red:

"Here, no one is too low to learn."

CHAPTER TWENTY-SIX

GHOSTS AND GARDENS

> *"This land remembers everything– The bullets and the lullabies. We grow what we can between them."*
>
> **– Dev,**
> **Postscript to The Soil That Sang**

In New Delhi, a storm of papers clattered inside the archives of the National Documentary Trust. Ranya Singh, 27, sharp-eyed and soft-voiced, dug through brittle footage reels and fading interviews with jungle insurgents. Her fingers trembled not from cold, but from legacy.

She was the granddaughter of Brigadier Ajit Singh–the man who had once ordered the Bastar jungle raids.

No one knew her lineage. Not yet. Not when she first saw Komal speaking at a university protest in Hyderabad. Not when she slipped into Bastar with a DSLR and a forged press card. And certainly not when she found herself seated across from Meera, now greying, still radiant with the fire of unfinished dreams.

"You're not with the news channels," Meera said.

"No. I'm... trying to understand what this all became."

"You won't find answers in a lens," Meera replied, sipping tamarind water. "You have to feel the soil where the blood dried."

Following Komal

Ranya shadowed Komal, the child of a slain tribal poet, now a lawyer and orator. Komal took her through ruined schoolhouses turned community halls, past murals of Arjun and Veena, to a tiny printshop where Dev still bound pamphlets by hand.

"These aren't just papers," Dev said. "They're kindling."

Ranya filmed everything. The broken crayons in the school that still bore Veena's initials. The banyan roots that wrapped around bullet-riddled walls. The red soil pressed into the hands of children chanting freedom songs.

She began calling her project *Red Soil, Burning Hearts.*

The Garden of Letters

On her final visit, Komal led her to a quiet hillside above Panchgaon, where rows of flowering saplings stood. Each one marked with a small wooden plaque bearing names: Veena, Arjun, Dev, unknown villagers, slain teachers.

"This is the Garden of Letters," Komal whispered. "Every name here once taught someone to speak against silence."

Ranya found Veena's grave–a hand-carved stone, vines curling gently over the base. She brushed the moss away. The words etched deep into stone:

"I taught them letters. They gave me legacy."

As the camera rolled, Ranya's voice cracked behind it. She turned it off.

And wept.

The Premiere

The premiere of *Red Soil, Burning Hearts* took place in the Critics' Corner at Cannes. Sparse attendance. Nervous silence.

But when Veena's final quote filled the screen, a journalist stood and asked, "Why did you make this film?"

Ranya paused. "Because I inherited violence... and I wanted to return it as truth."

The applause was not thunderous. But it was honest.

Back in Panchgaon, villagers watched the same film projected against a white bedsheet under the stars. Meera, sitting beside Komal and Dev, whispered:

"He died. But not quietly."

Komal placed her hand on Meera's.

"No," she said. "He became a garden."

CHAPTER TWENTY-SEVEN

ECHOES IN THE CAPITAL

> *"The capital heard gunfire as static, protests as wind, and hunger as rumour."*
>
> **– Meera, Interview**

The footage went viral.

The screams, the smoke, the slogans painted on broken walls. Parliament roared with debate. Anchor desks rattled with righteous fury and cautious spins.

But then came a face. Not Arjun's. Not Meera's. But the face of a young Member of Parliament – Radhika Sen – standing on the floor of the Lok Sabha, her voice trembling, her fists clenched.

She wore a white sari with a black armband.

"They told my father he died a patriot," she said. "But he died a pawn. Arjun was never our enemy. He was what this nation refused to listen to."

The chamber fell into stunned silence. On one side of the aisle, old men shifted uneasily. On the other hand, younger MPs stared at her like someone had cracked open a locked tomb.

Outside, protests surged.

At JNU, students draped red scarves around the Mahatma statue.

At Jamia, walls bloomed with graffiti:

"If memory bleeds, let it flood."

At the gates of Parliament, thousands gathered. Some with signs that read *Justice for Forgotten Forests*, others holding portraits of Arjun, Veena, Tara.

And atop a cement block, arms outstretched and voice ringing like a bell in the monsoon – Komal.

Veena's former student.

Now a firebrand, barefoot and fearless.

"This is not about revenge," Komal shouted. "It's about memory. It's about reclaiming the country they buried under cement and silence. History does not erase. It returns!"

The crowd roared.

A candle lit in Bastar had become a blaze in the capital.

And deep within a committee chamber, someone whispered: "Maybe it's time we rewrite the textbooks."

CHAPTER TWENTY-EIGHT

THE SEEDS AND THE SONG

> *"We once sowed fire into the soil. Now we bury seeds with gentler hands, and sing–not of war, but of what must grow after it. Even in silence, our soil remembers the tune, While the seed waits for rain"*
>
> **– Meera, Interview**

The documentary team arrived just after the rains, stepping lightly across the softened battlefield soil. The site–once the heart of a firefight–now breathed in chlorophyll and children's laughter. Where blood had dried into memory, hands now broke ground to plant life.

A drone hovered above, recording from the sky as dozens of village children dug small holes with their fingers. Saplings were passed down a human chain–neem, banyan, mango. Each planted not just to grow, but to remember.

Komal moved among them, humming a tune under her breath.

"Dig with your hands, dig with your heart, let freedom rise from where they buried art."

The words stirred the breeze.

One of the filmmakers zoomed in, curious. "What is that song?" she asked Komal.

Komal smiled, wiping her hands on her skirt. "It was Arjun's. Written during the war. Before a night raid."

[Years Earlier]

Smoke curled above the campfire like a warning no one heeded. Arjun sat hunched over a page half-burned from the last ambush. Ink had run out days ago. Now he dipped a twig into charcoal-soaked tea.

Across from him, Veena and Meera plotted supply routes over a crumpled map. Dev snored with a book on his chest.

Arjun scribbled:

"Dig with your hands…"

He paused. Looked up at the canopy above–the same sky that had seen his uncle hanged, his classroom burned, his teacher humiliated.

He thought of the girl with a slate broken in half, still trying to trace her name. He thought of Veena's shawl billowing like defiance.

"Dig with your heart…"

A tear smudged the line. He wiped it quickly.

Veena looked over. "Writing?"

He nodded.

"Good," she whispered. "They burn our books. We sing ours."

[Present Day – Documentary Scene]

In the village clearing, the song returned–not just in Komal's voice, but in the children's chorus, lifting into the lens of the drone like a prayer.

"Let freedom rise from where they buried art…"

The filmmakers caught the moment: children planting saplings, red thread tied around trunks, verses pinned to leaves with clothes pegs.

Komal knelt beside a neem tree and buried a small object–an old cassette tape, labelled in fading ink: *Arjun – Final Recording.*

"To grow, we must bury–not to forget, but to remember differently," she told the camera.

The team later filmed Meera at the People's Canopy, reciting lines from Arjun's diary. Her voice cracked on one entry:

"We wrote songs not to win–but to last longer than the guns."

That evening, the documentary crew packed up. The drone caught its final shot: children dancing barefoot around saplings, each singing Arjun's song.

Beneath the surface, roots spread. Above them, verses floated into the air like dandelion seeds.

And history, once written in ash and blood, now grew in leaves.

CHAPTER TWENTY-NINE

KOMAL'S TORCH (NEW GENERATION)

> *"They thought the fire had died. But Komal arrived with smoke in her breath, and matches in her pocket."*
>
> **– Dev,**
> **Last Broadcast from JanSwar Press**

Komal remembered Meera not as a warrior, but as a woman who wiped her tears with chalk-dusted hands.

Now, years later, Komal stood in front of a repurposed community hall in the heart of the red zone, renamed Azadi Nagar. What was once a police outpost now bore murals of tribal gods, freedom fighters, and lines from Arjun's diary.

She led a sprawling underground education movement known as *Gyan Mukti* – Freedom Through Knowledge. The schools, often hidden in clearings or caves, taught tribal languages, resistance literature, history censored by official syllabi, and the Constitution. There were classes on soil chemistry and guerrilla agriculture, poetry workshops, and first-aid combat training.

In one such moonlit grove, a group of children and teenagers sat cross-legged on the forest floor. Fireflies glowed like scattered embers. A bamboo torch crackled at the centre.

Komal walked among them barefoot, carrying a wooden slate engraved with the preamble of the Constitution.

"They made our ancestors kneel," she said, voice steady, "but you – you will teach their grandchildren to stand."

The students repeated it, some unsure, some proud:

"We will teach them to stand."

"Good," she smiled. "Now, who can tell me what Article 21A guarantees?"

A girl no older than nine stood up.

"Right to education," she said. "For every child. No matter what."

Komal knelt beside her. "And who denied you that right?"

The girl answered softly: "The school that closed when the land was sold. The police who burned our books."

Above them, a drone buzzed faintly in the dark sky. A surveillance pattern they had all grown used to. But Komal looked up, unfazed.

"Let them watch," she said. "Let them learn what liberation looks like."

Later that night, she sat alone beside an old banyan stump. She placed a candle at its base and whispered:

"Veena, they remember. And they write their names in your ink."

The banyan, long burned, now cradled a sapling in its crook – its first leaf red with soil, the shape of a heart.

The revolution had children now. And they carried torches instead of guns.

CHAPTER THIRTY

RAIPUR RECKONING

> *"A reckoning doesn't knock on the door. It walks in barefoot, with names buried. And refuses to leave."*
>
> **– Meera,**
> **testimony transcript (excerpt)**

The newsroom lights flickered as Dev watched the footage for the hundredth time. It was the final cut of *Red Soil, Burning Heart*, the segment where Veena's students chant under monsoon skies, where Arjun's last words bleed across a canvas of fire and banyan roots.

Each time he watched, something broke. And something else rose.

Outside his printshop-turned-refugee press office in Raipur, the sirens of the state blared louder. Arrests had begun. Editors detained; activists smeared. The crackdown was swift and brutal.

Inside, Dev opened his rusted laptop, the keys worn, the battery flickering between life and surrender. He began typing, not for fame, not even for memory. But for accountability.

"To betray a cause once is human. To atone for it forever is revolutionary."

The piece was titled *Reckoning in Red.* He submitted it to JanSwar, the last surviving underground outlet.

Minutes later, a low pain coiled around his chest. He reached for the inhaler. Missed.

The screen glowed one last time. Then black.

The Wake

By morning, the story had gone viral.

#DevLives trended in five languages.

Journalists lit candles outside media houses. Former enemies–from bureaucrats to civil society heads–issued statements of mourning. But in Bastar, grief came without pretence.

Meera sat beside his body, stroking his hair like a mother would. Komal wept without sound, her fists clenched around a crumpled copy of Dev's first banned poem: *Truth is a River.*

A pyre was built near the banks of the Indravati. Thousands gathered–tribal elders, students in red scarves, ex-militants, forest teachers, even repentant police officers. Silence fell like dusk.

Aftermath

His ashes were scattered across three places: the banyan roots of Panchgaon, the press ruins in Raipur, and the blackboards of Veena's school.

Meera placed his last printed column in a sealed jar beneath the banyan tree.

"His words will grow back," she said.

The JanSwar server crashed due to traffic. Komal and others archived Dev's writings into an encrypted repository called *The Archive of Flame.*

In Raipur, a youth-led march erupted without warning. Placards bore lines from Dev's columns:

- *Journalism is rebellion in ink.*
- *Don't publish news. Publish nerve.*

Three weeks later, the Chief Minister referenced Dev's legacy in the Assembly.

But in the jungle, Komal read aloud one final entry Dev had typed but never sent:

"They can erase my name. Not the fires I lit."

She folded the paper. Burned it.

Let it rise.

His funeral was attended by thousands–activists, tribal leaders, repentant officials.

Komal lit his pyre with a line from his banned poem:

"Smoke cannot lie. It rises only from fire."

CHAPTER THIRTY-ONE

THE FINAL WHISPER

> *"Not every revolution ends in thunder. Some end in a breath–just loud enough for the right ears to carry it forward."*
>
> **– Meera,**
> **closing lines of the Interview**

A joint operation was launched. Over 500 CRPF, State Police, and hired informants. Helicopters buzzed above the canopy.

Betrayal came from *Comrade Dev*, a soft-spoken mole in their ranks, who sold their location for a government posting.

It was in the Bhairavpur hills where hell came.

The forest exploded with bullets. Birds screamed. Trees caught fire. Arjun led the defence, firing with a broken shoulder, blood blinding his left eye. Six comrades fell. Three survived. The ridge was held–then lost.

Rain fell softly as dawn crawled in. Arjun inspected their trenches. The enemy approached from the east. Helicopters thrummed above.

He turned to his unit.

"If we die today, die knowing they feared our memory."

Veena kissed him. "Make them remember the kiss of the soil."

Lalu raised the flag. "My father was silenced. I am the echo."

The first bullet came at 6:47 AM.

Arjun fired three in return. Two landed.

Smoke. Screams. Traps triggered–a few vehicles flipped by an improvised explosive. The rebels sang as they fired.

Dev watched from afar, trembling, guilt swallowing his spine. "I am the storm I betrayed."

Arjun was shot in the shoulder. Still, he charged. "Veena! Grenade the flank!"

She pulled both pins, shouted, "Fly, my sparrow!" and dove into the brush.

He handed a letter to Meera, and Lalu left from there for Meera.

Arjun collapsed behind a fallen log. Veena's blood soaked his shirt.

Arjun, broken and bleeding, was carried into a limestone cave behind a waterfall. He drifted between life and death. Meera, along with Lalu, came to him a few hours later, carrying nothing but a satchel of herbs, a prayer, and a pencil.

He smiled through cracked lips. "It's time," he whispered.

From beneath his cot, he pulled a red diary. "Guard this. It holds our tomorrow."

"I've written it all–every lie, every crime. Let them read. Let them *remember*."

That night, Meera sang a Gondi lullaby as he faded into stillness, *his blood soaked into the stone like roots.*

Meera left for the tribal hamlet of Bhairavpur at dusk, her jeep covered in the reddish dust that clung like the blood of memory.

CHAPTER THIRTY-TWO

MEMORY CAMPS

> *"They built these camps to break us. We returned to build memory in their ruins. Now every brick remembers a name."*
>
> **– Meera,**
> **during the Interview at the Memory Camp**

In the vast clearings where once military boots stamped out resistance, the government had erected Memory Camps. Gone were the barbed wires and camouflage. In their place stood open-air shelters with bamboo walls and roofs thatched in palm leaves – spaces shaped by the people, for the people.

Each camp held exhibits – torn saris recovered from raid sites, schoolbooks half-burned, bullets marked with numbers. On one wall, a mural depicted Arjun carrying a torch made of script and fire. Another showed Veena in front of a blackboard, surrounded by children whose shadows formed rifles – but only shadows.

Meera, now older and thinner but with fire still behind her eyes, moved from camp to camp, curating stories. She helped survivors record oral testimonies in tribal dialects. Each story was filed – not for prosecution, but for preservation.

In Camp *Koylibeda*, a young boy stepped onto the open dais. On his shirt was a hand-stitched name: ARJUN.

He opened a tattered red diary and began to read:

"A bullet can kill a rebel. But not the idea he wrote in red."

The crowd grew still. Elders wiped their eyes. A mother in the back clutched her daughter tighter.

At another camp in Dantewada, children performed reenactments of the Night of Ashes. They did not use real fire – only flickering lanterns and blackened cloths. When they mimed the soldiers burning the grain, one girl stood defiantly before them and shouted:

"You cannot starve the seeds of memory!"

Afterward, a survivor named Leela, once a combat medic in the forest, told her story.

"They told us we were vermin. That forests don't breed humans. But I bled. I healed. I taught my comrades to do the same."

She showed a photograph: young Arjun, holding a wounded man and smiling. "He didn't just fight. He listened."

The camps were not monuments to vengeance. They were gardens of collective grief. In one corner, women planted red hibiscus – one for every life lost during 'Operation Dhwast'. A small plaque read:

"Flowers for the silenced. Voices for the unborn."

UN observers visited. A young delegate from South Africa whispered to Meera:

"Your rebels speak like poets."

Meera answered:

"They were made by fire. But they chose to burn with meaning."

In the twilight of one such evening, Komal arrived with students from *Gyan Mukti*. They sat beneath a banyan sapling – grown from a seed smuggled out before the Witness Tree fell.

Komal touched the leaves and whispered:

"Your memory is soil. And we are your rain."

The Memory Camps were not just a reckoning.

They were howwounded people remembered – and grew back roots in their own names.

CHAPTER THIRTY-THREE

MEERA'S NEW LESSON

> *The revolution taught us how to fight. Now I teach them how to live beyond it."*
>
> **– Meera,**
> **first day at the rebuilt school**

Meera began teaching history again–this time in the village she once defended with rage.

The classroom had no walls.

It stood in the shade of the same banyan sapling planted in the Memory Camp. Birds trilled among its branches. Children sat in a wide circle on mats made from jute sacks stitched by former prisoners.

Meera arrived barefoot, as always. Her sari was frayed but spotless. She carried no books–only a single wooden slate, polished from use.

"Today's lesson," she said, "isn't from a textbook."

She wrote on the slate with chalk: *TRUTH.*

A girl raised her hand. "Is that a story?"

Meera smiled gently. "It's many. Told by people who weren't believed. Or buried before they could speak."

A boy with a scar down his temple stood up. "Like my mother? They said she lied when she screamed."

Meera nodded; her voice steady. "Then scream with her voice. Sing what they tried to erase."

She gave each child a seed – mahua, neem, tamarind – and asked them to write one truth on paper and bury it beneath the tree.

"We plant memory," she said, "so even if we vanish, the forest will remember."

In the afternoons, elders came to sit among the children. They told stories of fire and rice, of how grief had once been outlawed.

At sunset, Meera lit a lantern and placed it at the banyan's base. "This light," she said, "is for those whose stories were too painful to speak. But we carry them now."

Her final assignment was always the same:

"Tell the truth. Even if no one listens. Especially when no one listens."

And each student, on the last day of class, was given a copy of Arjun's diary.

Inside the cover, in Meera's handwriting:

"This is your beginning, not your end."

CHAPTER THIRTY-FOUR

THE LAST LETTER

> *"I do not know if this letter will reach you– But if it does, let it carry what my voice no longer can: That I never stopped believing in what we began. This letter is not a goodbye."*
>
> **– Veena,**
>
> **final letter to Meera (undelivered)**

While unpacking books donated by villagers for the new library, Komal found a torn satchel that once belonged to Veena. Inside its lining, worn thin by time and forest dust, was a folded piece of cloth paper sealed with twine.

She untied it gently. Inside was a letter, written in Veena's unmistakable script:

"To whoever finds this: Teach them to read my silence. It holds more truth than my screams ever did. –Veena."

Komal clutched it to her chest. That night, under lantern light, she read it aloud to the library builders – masons, farmers, schoolgirls, a few retired fighters.

They wept silently, not from sadness, but recognition.

Komal had the letter framed, not with glass, but in raw wood, hung in the heart of the new library. Below it, a quote painted in tribal script:

“Words once buried are now seeds.”

The library was named *Veena Smriti Ghar* – The House of Veena’s Memory.

And children came, not to forget war, but to remember how to turn silence into speech.

CHAPTER THIRTY-FIVE

FOREST PARLIAMENT

> *"Power does not always rise from marble floors. Sometimes, it grows from roots, And speaks in the language of those who were never asked."*
>
> **– Komal,**
> **on the making of a people's constitution**

In the eerie remnants of a once foreboding paramilitary stronghold, the atmosphere buzzed with a new energy. The walls, once marred by the violence of gunfire and the sharp commands of commanding officers, now embraced a gentler vibe, adorned with intricately woven bamboo mats and lovingly crafted tapestries that told stories of resilience and transformation.

Leaders from different scattered tribal clans gathered around a short wooden table, their faces covered with earth colours and ash. Age and wisdom showed in their wrinkles; youth shone in their eyes. There were no ranks here–only roles earned by trust and service.

Komal, now known not just as an educator but as a convener, opened the meeting.

"We gather not as soldiers or survivors, but as stewards. Today, we talk not of war, but of life."

Sitting around the circle was the Healer, whose hands had healed spiritual as well as bodily injuries. Beside her, the Protector–who had formerly carried weapons–now carried the weight of preserving peace. The Storyteller carried a carved wooden staff, her voice poised to entwine their history. Komal's eyes met each delegate. "Our forest is home, our culture a flame that must not be extinguished."

The first motion was clear, born from years of blood and soil:

"We declare the Red Belt a Protected Lifestyle Zone."

Voices rose in agreement–some loud, some quiet, but all resolute.

"This land is not for conquest," said the Elder. "It is for living, for learning, for remembering."

The motion passed unanimously.

Far beyond the forest, in the halls of Parliament, the government echoed the same declaration–legally recognizing the Red Belt as a Protected Lifestyle Zone, a sanctuary for tribal life, culture, and the forest's fragile ecology.

Outside, the forest seemed to lean in, branches swaying gently as if in approval.

Here, in this reclaimed bunker, the future was no longer written with bullets, but with promises.

The Forest Parliament had begun.

CHAPTER THIRTY-SIX

THE STATUE CRACKS

The monsoon came early that year, like a long-awaited sigh over the scarred land of Bastar. Thunder rolled over the hills with a voice like old gods returning, and the skies split open with the kind of rage only memory can summon.

In the heart of Panchgoan, the statue of Arjun stood tall–chiselled from black basalt, his eyes cast forward, his fist raised, not in violence, but in memory. Below, etched on stone:

"Leaders do not die. They multiply."

Villagers often left red hibiscus flowers at its base. Children played tag around it. Protestors paused to touch its feet like pilgrims.

But on that storm-soaked morning, lightning struck.

It didn't come gently. It carved through the sky like a divine blade and cleaved the statue clean down the centre–splitting Arjun's likeness into two halves. The sound echoed across the valley like a verdict.

Gasps spread. Some wept. Others stared in disbelief.

But Meera, older now, wrapped in a faded red shawl, stepped forward. She placed a hand on the fractured torso, its stone heart exposed.

"Do not grieve," she said, her voice steady beneath the rumble of thunder. "He never wanted to be worshipped. Only remembered. And so, he was. Forever, in this red soil.

The villagers listened. Then, one by one, they approached the broken statue and began taking small pieces–not as relics, but as seeds.

A mother placed a fragment at the base of the old banyan–the People's Canopy.

A boy carried one to the village school and set it beside the blackboard.

An elder tied a shard with red thread and hung it from the eaves of his home.

And deep in the jungle, Komal planted hers beneath the roots of a neem tree and whispered, "Grow from this."

The statue, once singular and towering, now became many–dispersed across the land, resting not above the people but among them. No longer a monument, but a memory carried like a wound and a weapon.

That night, Meera sat beneath the storm-cleansed sky, reading from Arjun's diary to a circle of children.

"We are not statues," she read aloud. "We are echoes. We are fire carried forward in breath."

In the soft dark, the trees swayed gently, as if nodding.

And from the cracks in stone, a new kind of legacy began to bloom.

CHAPTER THIRTY-SEVEN

THE DEBATE OF ASHES

The morning after the storm, the village gathered beneath the old banyan–no longer just a tree, but a testament. Elders, teachers, students, and former rebels sat in a circle, the air thick with monsoon steam and memory. At the centre, a single stone shard from Arjun's shattered statue rested on folded red cloth–neither relic nor debris, but a question.

"We must rebuild it," said a young teacher. "The children need to see him whole."

An elder woman, her voice dry as cracked bark, replied, "Statues cast shadows. Memory moves in light."

A former fighter rose; his voice still edged with fire. "He was our general, our shield. Our story. Let the world see that we remember."

Komal stood with arms crossed, her gaze steady. "The world already sees. But do we understand what he stood for?"

Meera remained quiet, her eyes on the stone. When the wind stirred the banyan leaves above, she finally spoke.

"If we raise him again, let it not be in granite. Let it be in syllables. In saplings. In syllabuses. Let children carry him in their questions, not just their eyes."

A girl–barefoot, no older than ten–stepped forward. She held up a wooden slate. On it, in red chalk, she had written a single word: *Arjun.*

"I don't need a statue," she said. "I have his name."

Silence fell–neither agreement nor dissent, only a shared breath.

And then, the elders nodded. No vote. Just consent carved in stillness.

They did not rebuild the statue.

Instead, they dug into the red soil and planted seeds where his feet once stood.

When spring came, it was not stone that rose–but wildflowers, red-leafed saplings, and birds that learned to sing his name into the morning air.

--------------THE NEW BEGINNING ---------------

RICE SOAKED IN BLOOD:

They counted names, but not our hunger cries,
measured castes with broken scale, while ignoring the flies.
Rice locked away in silent government sacks,
as our bones grew sharp against our backs.

A mother pleaded with empty hands,
only to hear that her name wasn't in the ledgers.
A child starved, a stone was thrown,
A dream burnt up in flames.

Then came the forces, blistered feet pounding the ground,
Our cries echoed from every street.
And bullets taught us the price of fate,
we felt them like summer rain,
while white rice soaked up with red-stained pain.

No priest, no flag, just smoke and mud,
and rice still steaming in the blood.
Rice simmered in pots across the land,
served with a trembling and calloused hand.

Now, every meal I touch
it tastes more of silence than of light.
And every grain in my plate
reminds me of who holds our fate.

ABOUT THE AUTHOR

Rahul Nandigam was born in Khammam, India. He began writing in childhood and has contributed to school and college magazines. He has lived in Hyderabad since childhood and is publishing his first novel, Red Soil, Burning Hearts.

Successful as a dental doctor, he achieved many milestones in his career. As a contribution, he developed a surgical procedure for providing better oral health to his patients. He is dedicating his time to writing a book on dentistry as a way to give back to his profession.

Rahul Nandigam is a true creative at heart, with a passion for writing and food. As a food enthusiast he along with his elder brother has launched healthy food snacks under brands 'Yumscoop' and 'Relish'. His artistic endeavours serve as a means of self-expression, allowing him to explore the world through different mediums. Rahul Nandigam's work tries to capture the beauty of everyday life, showcasing the exceptional in the ordinary.

'Red Soil, Burning Hearts' is truly inspired by the fact that as a growing child in his family, he heard about the struggles and social justice and system in the society. He tried to capture this in the most sensitive manner in this story so that this generation and coming generations can know what has happened in history, which can lead to some motivation.

He feels truly, greatly thankful for his parents, his elder brother and paternal uncle, who has inspired him, supported him and encouraged him in this new phase of his life as a writer, bringing his first book into publication and realising his dream.